THIS BOOK BELONGS TO

**HIGH LIFE
HIGHLAND**

3800 13 0060148 5	
Askews & Holts	Nov-2013
JF	£12.99

First published in hardback in Great Britain by HarperCollins Children's Books in 2013

1 3 5 7 9 10 8 6 4 2

ISBN: 978-0-00-742508-2

HarperCollins Children's Books is a division of HarperCollins Publishers Ltd.

Text and illustrations copyright © Emma Chichester Clark 2013

Text abridged by Alison Sage and retold by Emma Chichester Clark

Visit our website at www.harpercollins.co.uk

Printed in China

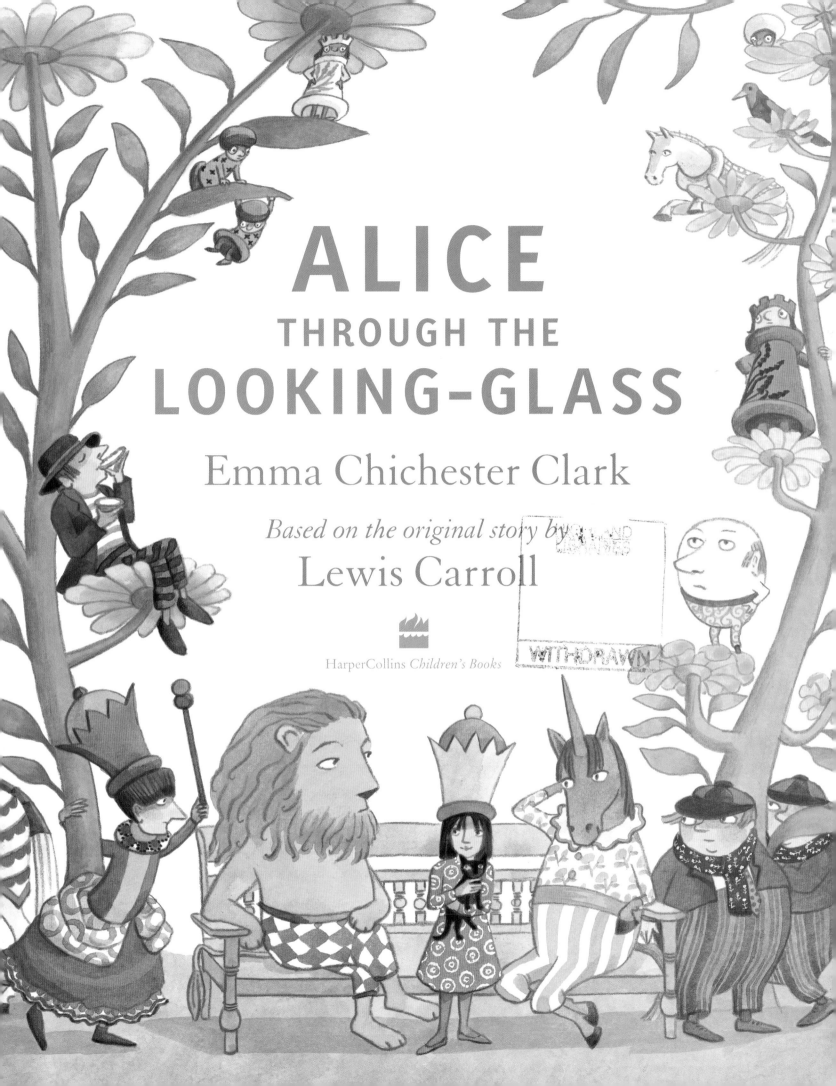

ALICE
THROUGH THE
LOOKING-GLASS

Emma Chichester Clark

Based on the original story by
Lewis Carroll

HarperCollins *Children's Books*

Snow was falling softly against the windowpanes and Alice was playing her favourite game of 'Let's pretend' with her little black kitten.

"Kitty, can you play chess?" she asked. "Let's pretend you're the Red Queen! If you sat up and folded your arms you'd look just like her. Look at you!"

She held the kitten up to the mirror.

"Oh, Kitty! How nice it would be if we could only get through into the Looking-glass House where everything is back to front! I'm sure it has such beautiful things in it! Let's pretend the glass has got all soft, so that we can get through…"

And, suddenly, like a bright silvery mist,

the glass began

to melt away…

In a moment, Alice found herself in the Looking-glass room. Instead of being like the old room she had come from, it was completely different. Everything, even the pictures, seemed to be alive and the chess pieces were walking about in pairs!

"Here are the Red King and Queen!" Alice whispered. "And the White King and Queen and two Castles walking arm in arm! I don't think they can hear me," she went on, "and I'm *sure* they can't see me!"

Beside her, on the table, a little white pawn rolled about, squeaking and kicking its legs in the air!

"It's the voice of my child!" cried the White Queen, looking up. "My precious Lily!"

Alice, anxious to help, knelt down and lifted the White Queen on to the table.

"What – was – that?" gasped the White Queen. The rapid journey through the air had quite taken her breath away.

Next Alice gently picked up the White King and put him beside the Queen but he fainted in astonishment.

"I shall *never* forget that!" he said eventually.

Meanwhile, Alice had found a book. It was written in a very strange language:

JABBERWOCKY

But when she held it up to the mirror, it all became clear.

"It's a Looking-glass book, so everything is back to front," thought Alice. "But, oh! I must hurry and see the garden before I have to go back!"

JABBERWOCKY

'Twas brillig, and the slithy toves
    Did gyre and gimble in the wabe;
All mimsy were the borogoves,
    And the mome raths outgrabe.

"Beware the Jabberwock, my son!
    The jaws that bite, the claws that catch!
Beware the Jubjub bird, and shun
    The frumious Bandersnatch!"

He took his vorpal sword in hand:
    Long time the manxome foe he sought –
So rested he by the Tumtum tree,
    And stood awhile in thought.

And as in uffish thought he stood,
    The Jabberwock, with eyes of flame,
Came whiffling through the tulgey wood,
    And burbled as it came!

One, two! One, two! And through and through
    The vorpal blade went snicker-snack!
He left it dead, and with its head
    He went galumphing back.

"And hast thou slain the Jabberwock?
    Come to my arms, my beamish boy!
A frabjous day! Callooh! Callay!"
    He chortled in his joy.

'Twas brillig, and the slithy toves
    Did gyre and gimble in the wabe;
All mimsy were the borogoves,
    And the mome raths outgrabe.

She seemed to float down the stairs and into the garden where she suddenly found herself face to face with the Red Queen (who had grown considerably).

"Where are you from and where are you going?" said the Red Queen. "Look up and speak nicely!"

"I'm finding my way around the garden…" began Alice.

"I don't know what you mean by *your* way!" said the Queen. "All ways about here belong to me!"

Alice looked at the view. There were squares everywhere. "It's just like a giant chessboard!" she said. "Oh, I wish I could join in! I'd love to be a Queen!"

"Well, you can! You're already on the Second Square," said the Red Queen. "You'll go by train through the Third – the Fourth belongs to Tweedledum and Tweedledee – the Fifth is over some water – and the Sixth belongs to Humpty Dumpty. The Seventh is all forest – a Knight will guide you – and in the Eighth Square we shall all be Queens together for a feast!"

The Queen took Alice's hand. "Faster! Faster!" she cried as they ran. "Don't try to talk!"

They skimmed through the air, the wind whistling in their ears, but when they stopped Alice was amazed to find they hadn't moved at all! "In *our* country," she said, "you'd generally get to somewhere else, after running."

But the Queen had vanished!

Before she had time to even think about the Red Queen, Alice found herself sitting in a train carriage. It was full of the strangest passengers.

"Tickets, please!" said the guard, staring angrily at Alice through a pair of binoculars.

"I'm afraid I haven't got one," Alice said nervously. "There wasn't a ticket office where I came from."

"Don't make excuses," said the guard.

"She ought to know her way to the ticket office, even if she doesn't know her alphabet!" said a goat.

"She ought to know her way, even if she doesn't know her own name!" said a man dressed entirely in white paper.

And the chorus of voices went on.

An extremely small voice sighed very close to Alice's ear. "I know you are a friend," it said, "a dear friend and an old one, and you won't hurt me, though I am an insect."

"What kind of insect?" asked Alice, turning around in vain to see it and hoping it wasn't one that might sting. But as it began to reply there was a shriek from the engine and everyone jumped in alarm.

"It's only a little stream we have to jump over," explained the horse. "It'll take us to the Fourth Square."

Alice was relieved to hear that, but was still a bit worried at the idea of the train jumping when, suddenly, it leapt in the air and in her panic, she grabbed the nearest thing to hand which happened to be the goat's beard!

Then the train and its passengers simply melted away.

Alice sat under a tree. The insect was gently fanning her with its wings. It was a very large Gnat: "about the size of a chicken!" thought Alice, but she no longer felt afraid.

The gnat started telling Alice the names of some other insects. "But further on in the wood, there are no names!" it said, which Alice remembered as she walked away into the cool shade of the trees.

"What a relief, after being so hot, to get into the – into the – into what? I'm sure I used to know!" she thought. "And what about my name? What is it? I'm sure it begins with an 'A'…"

Rocking-horse-fly

Snap-dragon-fly

Bread-and-butter-fly

Just then a little fawn appeared and walked with Alice until they reached a clearing where, all at once, they both immediately remembered everything! The fawn looked at Alice with terror in its eyes and raced away at top speed.

"Oh, well," thought Alice. "At least I know who I am again!" She wandered on, talking to herself, until she saw two signposts, one saying 'Tweedledum', the other, 'Tweedledee'.

Turning a sharp corner Alice saw two fat little men dressed like schoolboys. They stood as still as statues. "Tweedledum and Tweedledee!" she thought, peering at them.

"If you think we're waxworks, you ought to pay, you know!" said Tweedledum.

"Could you tell me how to get out of this wood and into the Fifth Square?" Alice asked politely.

"You've begun wrong!" cried Tweedledum. "The first thing in a visit is to say 'How d'ye do?' and shake hands!"

Alice took both their hands at once, so as not to offend one by choosing the other first, but the next moment they were dancing around in a circle with music coming from the trees. The branches were playing themselves like violins. When it stopped, the brothers were gasping for breath.

"So, tell me," said Alice, "which way is the best way?"

But instead of answering, Tweedledee began to recite the longest poem he could think of…

"The sun was shining on the sea,
　　Shining with all his might:
He did his very best to make
　　The billows smooth and bright –
And this was odd, because it was
　　The middle of the night.

The moon was shining sulkily,
　　Because she thought the sun
Had got no business to be there
　　After the day was done –
'It's very rude of him,' she said,
　　'To come and spoil the fun!'

The sea was wet as wet could be,
　　The sands were dry as dry.
You could not see a cloud, because
　　No cloud was in the sky:
No birds were flying overhead –
　　There were no birds to fly.

The Walrus and the Carpenter
　　Were walking close at hand;
They wept like anything to see
　　Such quantities of sand:
'If this were only cleared away,'
　　They said, 'it would be grand!'

'If seven maids with seven mops
　　Swept it for half a year,
Do you suppose,' the Walrus said,
　　'That they could get it clear?'
'I doubt it,' said the Carpenter,
　　And shed a bitter tear.

'O Oysters, come and walk with us!'
　　The walrus did beseech,
'A pleasant walk, a pleasant talk,
　　Along the briny beach:
We cannot do with more than four,
　　To give a hand to each.'

The eldest Oyster looked at him.
　　But never a word he said:
The eldest Oyster winked his eye,
　　And shook his heavy head –
Meaning to say he did not choose
　　To leave the oyster-bed.

But four young oysters hurried up,
　　All eager for the treat:
Their coats were brushed, their faces washed,
　　Their shoes were clean and neat –
And this was odd, because, you know,
　　They hadn't any feet.

Four other Oysters followed them,
　　And yet another four;
And thick and fast they came at last,
　　And more, and more, and more –
All hopping through the frothy waves,
　　And scrambling to the shore.

The Walrus and the Carpenter
　　Walked on a mile or so,
And then they rested on a rock
　　Conveniently low:
And all the little Oysters stood
　　And waited in a row.

'The time has come,' the Walrus said,
　　'To talk of many things:
– Of shoes and ships – and sealing-wax –
　　Of cabbages – and kings –
And why the sea is boiling hot –
　　And whether pigs have wings.'

'But wait a bit,' the Oysters cried,
    'Before we have our chat;
For some of us are out of breath,
    And all of us are fat!'
'No hurry!' said the Carpenter.
    They thanked him much for that.

'A loaf of bread,' the Walrus said,
    'Is what we chiefly need:
Pepper and vinegar besides
    Are very good indeed –
Now if you're ready, Oysters dear,
    We can begin to feed.'

'But not on us!' the Oysters cried,
    Turning a little blue,
'After such kindness, that would be
    A dismal thing to do!'
'The night is fine,' the Walrus said.
    'Do you admire the view?

'It was so kind of you to come!
    And you are very nice!'
The Carpenter said nothing but
    'Cut us another slice:
I wish you were not quite so deaf –
    I've had to ask you twice!'

'It seems a shame,' the Walrus said,
    'To play them such a trick,
After we've brought them out so far,
    And made them trot so quick!'
The Carpenter said nothing but
    'The butter's spread too thick!'

'I weep for you,' the Walrus said,
    'I deeply sympathise.'
With sobs and tears he sorted out
    Those of the largest size,
Holding his pocket-handkerchief
    Before his streaming eyes.

'O Oysters,' said the Carpenter,
    'You've had a pleasant run!
Shall we be trotting home again?'
    But answer came there none –
And this was scarcely odd, because
    They'd eaten every one."

"What very unpleasant characters!" said Alice.

She was about to say goodbye and find her own way out of the wood when Tweedledum seized her by the wrist.

"Do you see that?" he screamed furiously, pointing at a small white thing lying under a tree.

"It's only an old, broken rattle," said Alice. "Not a rattle*snake*, you know!"

"But it was *new*!" roared Tweedledum. "I only bought it yesterday!" He stamped his foot and glared at Tweedledee who was desperately trying to hide inside an umbrella. "Of course you agree to have a battle?" Tweedledum asked his brother in a calmer tone.

"I suppose so," said Tweedledee sulkily. "Only *she* must help us dress up."

So the two went off, hand in hand, and reappeared with their arms full of extraordinary things – duvets, blankets, pots and pans, rugs and more.

"I hope you're good at pinning and tying!" said Tweedledum. "Every one of these things must go on, somehow or other!"

"These two will look more like bundles of old clothes by the time they're ready!" Alice said to herself.

"Let's fight until six, then have dinner!" said Tweedledum.

But it was suddenly getting terribly dark.

"What a thick, black cloud that is," thought Alice. "And how fast it comes! Why I do believe it's got wings!"

"It's the crow!" cried Tweedledum.

As Alice ran under a tree, the two brothers ran off as fast as their fat little legs would carry them.

Suddenly a shawl blew by. "Whose is this?" wondered Alice, catching it. And in another moment, the White Queen came running wildly through the woods.

"May I help you with your shawl?" asked Alice.

"I don't know what's the matter with it!" said the Queen. "It's in a temper! There's no pleasing it, whatever I do!"

Alice gently rearranged the shawl for the Queen and tried to tidy her hair, which was in a dreadful state.

"My brush has got entangled in it," sighed the Queen. "And I lost my comb yesterday."

"You should really have a lady's maid," suggested Alice.

"I'll take you with pleasure!" said the Queen. "Two pence a week and jam every other day!"

Alice laughed. "I didn't mean *me* and I don't want jam today!"

"The rule is jam tomorrow and jam yesterday but never jam today!" said the Queen as she stuck a plaster on her finger. "*Oh! Oh! Oh!* My finger's bleeding!" Then she pinned a brooch on her shawl and pricked her finger.

"It's very confusing," said Alice.

"That's how living backwards works!" the Queen smiled.

Just then a sudden gust of wind snatched up the shawl again and blew it over a little stream and into the Fifth Square.

Alice and the Queen raced after it.

"Is your finger better now?" asked Alice.

"Much be-e-t-ter! Be-etter! Be-e-e-hh!" the Queen bleated, now suddenly wrapped in wool and looking just like a sheep!

Alice rubbed her eyes. She seemed to be standing in a shop – and was that really a *sheep*, knitting, behind the counter? The shelves were completely crammed with things but they moved about as soon as Alice looked at them!

"What is it that you want to buy?" asked the sheep.

"I'd like to look all round first, please," said Alice.

"You can't look *all* round you," said the sheep, "unless you've got eyes in the back of your head!"

"Well, I'd like to buy an egg, please," said Alice.

The sheep took her money. "You must get it yourself!" she said and she went to the back of the shop and set an egg upright on a shelf.

Alice felt her way through the darkness, past tables and chairs that were growing branches, towards the egg, which only seemed to grow further and further away.

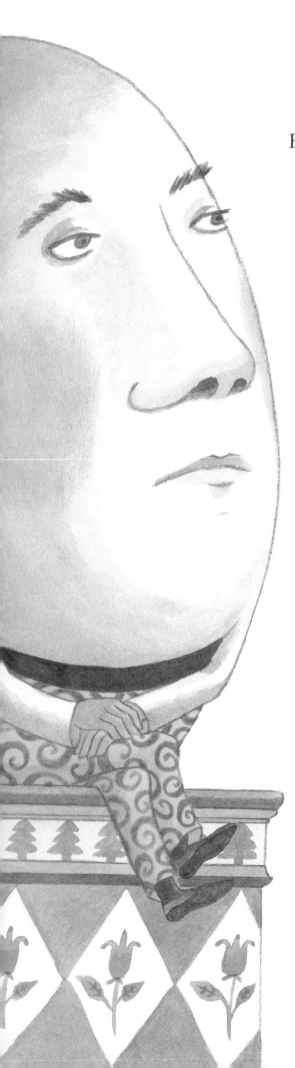

But at last, in the Sixth Square, Alice caught up with the egg. And it wasn't just any egg. It was Humpty Dumpty himself! He sat on a high wall, staring into the distance.

"You look just like an egg," said Alice. "And some eggs are very pretty you know."

Humpty Dumpty looked away. "Some people have no more sense than a baby," he muttered.

Alice didn't quite know what to say next so she sang softly:

"Humpty Dumpty sat on a wall.
Humpty Dumpty had a great fall.
All the King's horses and all the King's men
Couldn't put Humpty together again."

"Don't chatter to yourself!" Humpty Dumpty said crossly.

"Wouldn't you be safer on the ground?" asked Alice.

"Of course not! The King promised to send all his horses and all his men if I fall," said Humpty Dumpty, "so I can sit here all I like."

Alice watched anxiously as he leant forwards, holding out his hand.

"Goodbye!" he said suddenly.

"Till we meet again," said Alice.

"I wouldn't know you if we met again," said Humpty Dumpty. "You're so exactly like other people."

"You might recognise my face," said Alice.

"That's the trouble. They're all the same. Two eyes, nose in the middle, mouth under. If the eyes went on the same side of the nose, or the mouth at the top, that would help…"

Humpty Dumpty shut his eyes.

Alice waited a little to see if he would speak again, and then she quietly walked away.

A moment later, the forest shook with a heavy crash…

Soldiers were running through the wood – so many, they were falling over each other. And there was the White King!

"I sent them all!" he told Alice. "All but Hatta and Haigha, my messengers. Can you see them on the road?"

"I see nobody there," replied Alice.

"Oh, I wish *I* had such good eyes," said the King, "to see Nobody!"

Suddenly, a messenger arrived, skipping strangely.

"Haigha!" cried the King. "What's happening in town?"

"I'll whisper it," said Haigha, cupping his hands. "THEY'RE AT IT AGAIN!"

The King jumped. "Do you call *that* a whisper?"

"Who are at it again?" asked Alice.

"The Lion and the Unicorn, of course," said the King. "And it's *my* crown they're fighting for! Let's go and see them."

They trotted off, Alice repeating the words of an old song to herself as she ran,

"The Lion and the Unicorn were fighting for the crown:
The Lion beat the Unicorn all round the town.
Some gave them white bread, some gave them brown;
Some gave them plum cake and drummed them out of town."

A great crowd had gathered, including Hatta, who was drinking tea, with tears pouring down his cheeks.

"He's only just out of prison and he hadn't finished his tea when he went in, so he's thirsty," Haigha whispered to Alice.

"How are they getting on with the fight?" asked the King.

"Well," Hatta sobbed. "The Lion and the Unicorn have both been down eighty-seven times!"

"Ten minutes allowed for refreshments!" announced the King. Hatta and Haigha rushed round with trays of white and brown bread.

"What – is – *this*?" asked the Unicorn, staring at Alice with an air of the deepest disgust.

"It's a child!" said Haigha. "We found it today!"

Just then the Lion joined them. Looking very tired and sleepy, he blinked at Alice. "What's *this*?" he roared.

"You'll never guess!" cried the Unicorn, before Alice could reply. "It's a fabulous monster!"

"Then hand out the cake, Monster!" growled the Lion, and they all sat down, squeezing the King between them.

"I should easily win now," said the Lion.

"I'm not so sure of that!" replied the Unicorn.

"Hurry up with the cake, Monster!" the Lion growled.

Alice was sawing away at it, but every time she cut a slice, it all joined up again!

"You don't know how to manage Looking-glass cakes! Hand it out first and cut it afterwards!" ordered the Unicorn.

Alice obediently offered the cake around.

"It's not fair!" cried the Unicorn. "The Monster has given the Lion twice as much as me!"

But before Alice could answer, drums began sounding. They were so deafening, she leapt to her feet in terror, and over a little stream into the Seventh Square.

After a while, the noise died down, but suddenly loud shouting startled Alice.

"Ahoy! Ahoy! Check!" A Red Knight came galloping towards her.

"You're my prisoner!" he cried as he tumbled off his horse.

Then, suddenly, a White Knight drew up at Alice's side.

"Ahoy! Ahoy! Check!" he cried, and he too, tumbled to the ground.

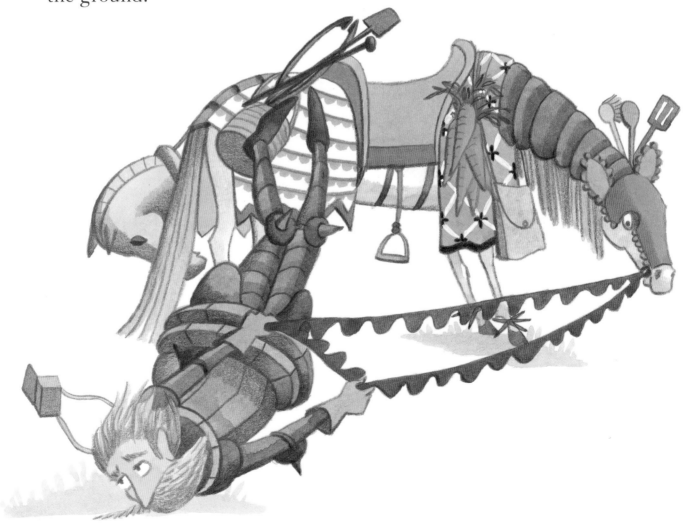

Both Knights remounted and glared at each other.

"We'll have to fight for her!" said the Red Knight, and they put on their helmets.

"You will, of course, observe the Rules of Battle?" asked the White Knight.

"I always do!" said the Red Knight, and they began bashing away at each other with their clubs.

It was hard for Alice to tell what the rules were – one seemed to be that they always fell on their heads, and this was how the battle ended.

Eventually they both got up, shook hands, and the Red Knight galloped away.

"It was a glorious victory, wasn't it?" the White Knight gasped.

"I don't know," said Alice doubtfully. "Anyway, I don't want to be a prisoner. I want to be a Queen!"

"But you will be!" said the Knight. "After you've crossed the next stream! I'll see you safely there."

While she was helping him out of his helmet, Alice noticed a little box tied round the Knight's neck.

"It's my own invention," said the Knight. "I keep it upside down to stop the rain getting in!"

"But things can get out," said Alice. "The lid's open!"

The Knight looked dismayed.

"And you've got a beehive…" said Alice, "and carrots…"

"It's as well to have everything!" answered the Knight. "And, you see, my horse has spikes round his hooves – to keep off the sharks!"

They walked on together. Each time the horse stopped, the Knight fell off and Alice helped him up again.

"I'm afraid you've not had much practice!" said Alice.

The Knight looked surprised. "What makes you say that?" he asked, as he scrambled back into the saddle, hanging on to a handful of Alice's hair, so as not to slide over the other side. "You've only got a few more steps to go now," he said, turning his horse's head. "But you'll stay and see me off?"

They shook hands and then the Knight rode away slowly, tumbling, first down one side of the horse, then the other. Alice waved her handkerchief until he was out of sight. Then she ran and jumped across the next stream.

"The Eighth Square at last!" she cried.

"Now to be a Queen!"

She landed on a soft, green lawn surrounded by flower beds.

"But what's *this*?" cried Alice, putting up her hands to find a heavy crown. "I never expected to be a Queen so soon!"

"Speak when you are spoken to!" snapped the Red Queen, appearing on one side of Alice, the White Queen on the other. Then the Red Queen turned to the White Queen, "I invite you to Alice's party!" she said.

"And I invite *you*!" replied the White Queen.

"I think *I* ought to invite the guests," said Alice.

But the other two Queens had fallen asleep with their heads in Alice's lap – and then they vanished!

"What am I to do?" wondered Alice. When she looked up, she saw a huge doorway with the words 'Queen Alice' above it. A creature with a long beak was watching her.

"No admittance till the week after next!" it said, slamming the door.

Alice kept knocking on the door until a very old frog, who'd been sitting under a tree, hobbled over.

"Shouldn't do that – shouldn't do that!" he muttered. "You let it alone and it'll let you alone, you know." And off he went.

At that moment, the door was flung open to the sound of loud singing and cheering, but as Alice entered, there was dead silence. At a long table sat all sorts of guests – birds, animals, and even a flower, with the Red Queen and the White Queen at one end. Alice sat down between them.

"You're late!" said the Red Queen. "Meet the mutton! Mutton – Alice! Alice – Mutton!"

The large leg of mutton stood up in its dish and bowed to Alice.

"Shall I carve it?" Alice asked anxiously.

"Certainly not!" replied the Red Queen. "You can't eat someone you've been introduced to!"

The mutton was then quickly replaced by a plum pudding.

"Pudding – Alice! Alice – Pudding!" said the Red Queen.

"I don't want to meet it," cried Alice, "or we'll never eat!"

"Let's drink to Queen Alice," said the Red Queen, "and then she'll make a speech!"

But as Alice began to speak, the two Queens started pushing her from either side until they'd almost lifted her over their heads.

"Take care!" cried the White Queen, grabbing Alice's hair. "Something's going to happen!"

And then the whole room went crazy…

The guests
were on the
table... the food
was flying about...
the bottles had wings
and whizzed through the
air... and the candles were
exploding like fireworks.

"Stop it at *once*!" cried Alice. "I can't stand this any longer!" She seized the edge of the tablecloth and gave it a good pull. Plates, dishes, guests and candles crashed down together in a heap on the floor.

Alice turned to the Red Queen, who seemed to be responsible for the chaos. "And as for *you*...!" she began, fiercely.

But the Queen was changing ... she was dwindling away, shrinking ... to the size of a kitten and was running round and round after her own shawl, which was trailing behind her. Alice held her up. The little creature went on shrinking! She was becoming shorter, fatter and softer, her eyes growing round and green, until she really *was* a kitten after all!

"Your Red Majesty shouldn't purr so loud," said Alice, putting down the little black kitten and rubbing her eyes. "Did you know that you've been with me in my dream in the Looking-glass world?"

The kitten just purred even more loudly as it washed its little paw.

"But was it *really* a dream?" Alice wondered. "After all, you were there – so you should know! Oh, Kitty! Why don't you answer me?"

But the naughty kitten only began on the other paw and pretended it hadn't heard the question.